D0438763

Purchased from
Multnomah County Library
Title Wave Used Bookstore
216 NE Knott St, Portland, OR
503-988-5021

Sly the Sleuth

and the Sports Mysteries

by Donna Jo Napoli and Robert Furrow

illustrated by Heather Maione

Dial Books for Young Readers

DIAL BOOKS FOR YOUNG READERS
A division of Penguin Young Readers Group
Published by The Penguin Group
Penguin Group (USA) Inc., 375 Hudson Street, New York, NY 10014, U.S.A.
Penguin Group (Canada), 90 Eglinton Avenue East, Suite 700, Toronto,
Ontario, Canada M4P 2Y3 (a division of Pearson Penguin Canada Inc.)
Penguin Books Ltd, 80 Strand, London WC2R 0RL, England
Penguin Ireland, 25 St. Stephen's Green, Dublin 2, Ireland
(a division of Penguin Books Ltd)
Penguin Group (Australia), 250 Camberwell Road, Camberwell, Victoria 3124,
Australia (a division of Pearson Australia Group Pty Ltd)
Penguin Books India Pvt Ltd, 11 Community Centre, Panchsheel Park,
New Delhi - 110 017, India
Penguin Group (NZ), Cnr Airborne and Rosedale Roads, Albany, Auckland
1310, New Zealand (a division of Pearson New Zealand Ltd)
Penguin Books (South Africa) (Pty) Ltd, 24 Sturdee Avenue, Rosebank,
Johannesburg 2196, South Africa
Penguin Books Ltd, Registered Offices: 80 Strand,
London WC2R 0RL, England

Text copyright © 2006 by Donna Jo Napoli and Robert Furrow
Illustrations copyright © 2006 by Heather Maione
The publisher does not have any control over and does not assume any
responsibility for author or third-party websites or their content.
All rights reserved
Designed by Jasmin Rubero
Text set in Bembo
Printed in the U.S.A.
1 3 5 7 9 10 8 6 4 2

Library of Congress Cataloging-in-Publication Data
Napoli, Donna Jo, date.
Sly the Sleuth and the sports mysteries / by Donna Jo Napoli and Robert
Furrow ; illustrated by Heather Maione.
p.   cm.
Summary: Sly uses her detective skills to help her friends solve
the case of the soccer switch, the kick craze, and the basketball blues.
ISBN 0-8037-2994-4
[1. Sports—Fiction. 2. Schools—Fiction. 3. Mystery and detective stories.]
I. Furrow, Robert, date. II. Maione, Heather Harms, ill. III. Title.
PZ7.N15Slg 2006
[Fic]—dc22
2005004817

Thanks to
Barry and Eva Furrow, Richard Tchen,
to Karen Riskin and Rebecca Waugh
and Lauri Hornik

Case #1:
Sly and the Soccer Switch

My Policies

I'm Sly the Sleuth. I run an agency called Sleuth for Hire. People bring me their problems. I solve them. So far I have solved every case.

My father says I should not get too cocky about it. Cocky people make mistakes. Plus, no one likes them. And he points out that I've only had three cases so far. They were all about pets. And they rhymed: the case of the Fat Cat, the case of the Wish Fish, and the case of the Frog Dog.

I'm not cocky. I'm just optimistic.

I like solving problems. It's fun.

That's one of my policies: I only take cases that are fun.

And only cases that a cat would care about. So when someone tells me a problem, I first ask myself what my cat, Taxi, would think.

These policies have never failed me yet. The cases I take make me happy.

I love being a sleuth.

Islands

My fourth case started with a bang.

Brian and I were sitting on the floor drawing. Brian is my neighbor. He goes to nursery school.

Bang! The porch door shook.

Brian jumped to his feet. "Earthquake!" he screamed.

"There are no earthquakes around here," I said.

Bang!

"Volcano!" screamed Brian.

"No volcanos either," I said.

Bang!

"Call the police," screamed Brian.

I opened the door.

A soccer ball hit me in the belly.

"Ouch," I said.

"Sorry." Jack fetched his ball and held it under one arm.

"Knocking is better," I said. "It's more traditional."

"I can't help it," said Jack. "I love to kick."

"I love to kick too," said Brian.

They both looked at me. I shrugged. "I

play baseball. Not a lot of kicking in baseball. What's up, Jack?"

"There's a problem."

"I knew it," said Brian. "Lava!" he
screamed.

"What's he talking about?" said Jack.

"What are you talking about, Brian?"

"Boom." Brian swung his arms over his
head. "Volcano, lava, islands. Water everywhere."

"Brian, has your teacher been talking
about how islands are formed?"

"We can get boats," said Brian. "I love boats. And Wilson will be happy. Islands are good for Wilson."

Wilson was Brian's name for all his frogs. He had a few dozen.

"How do you do that?" said Jack. "How do you figure out what Brian's talking about?"

"I've had a lot of practice," I said.

"And you're good at that sort of thing," said Jack. "That's why you can solve my case."

Mistakes

I went to the kitchen drawer. That's where I keep my sharpest pencil and my special pad of paper. Those are tools of the trade.

"Start at the beginning," I said.

"Soccer," said Jack.

Soccer is not my idea of fun. And Taxi hates soccer balls.

I put the pencil and pad back in the drawer.

"Go talk to your coach."

"Coach is baffled too," said Jack.

"Baffled?" said Brian.

"Confused," I said to Brian.

"Baffled booffled," said Brian.

"Go back to your drawing," I said.

I sat on the floor, picked up my pen, and went back to my own drawing.

"I need your help," said Jack.

"I don't know anything about soccer."

"I do," said Brian. "I know everything."

My drawing was homework. And I wasn't going to finish it if Brian kept talking and Jack didn't leave.

I went back into the kitchen. I filled a bowl with brownies. I filled another bowl with grapes. I held both bowls in front of Brian.

Brian stuffed a brownie in his mouth.

I knew he would. His mother makes only health foods.

I held the bowls in front of Jack.

Jack stuffed grapes in his mouth. Then he stuffed brownies in his pockets.

"What are you doing?" I said.

"I might get hungry later," said Jack. "You never know. Or I can sell them."

Jack was always short of money.

"It's not nice to sell other people's food," I said.

"You offered," said Jack. "So it's mine now. What's that?" He frowned at my drawing.

"Birds," I said. "It's homework. Haven't you had art class yet this week? The new art teacher is crazy about birds."

"If it's homework, why are you using a pen? Ink doesn't erase."

"That's the whole point. We're not supposed to think of stray marks as mistakes. We're supposed to think of them as opportunities."

Jack pointed. "That looks like a mistake to me."

"Go away now, Jack."

"You make a lot of mistakes, Sly. You're making a mistake not to take my case. Taxi would love it."

Friends

"Okay," I said. "I'll take the bait. Why would Taxi love your case?"

"I'll show you," said Jack. "Come."

"Where?"

"The soccer field."

Brian grabbed his green crayon and scribbled on his paper. "This is a soccer field."

I gathered Brian's crayons and stuck them in his backpack. Then I rolled his picture up and put it in too. I handed Brian his backpack. "See you later."

Brian left.

Jack ran ahead of me on the sidewalk, dribbling his soccer ball.

I caught up with him at the corner. We crossed together. Jack ran ahead again. He passed his house and jumped and waved. I wasn't surprised that he jumped. Jack jumps a lot. But the wave was a puzzle.

"Who are you waving at?" I called.

"Wish Fish," called back Jack.

I squinted at Jack's window. Yup, that was a fishbowl on the sill. And I could even make out Wish Fish's scarlet body.

"Hey, wait," came a voice from behind.

I turned around.

Melody raced up with Pong on a leash. Melody is my best friend. Pong is her puppy.

"Want to walk with us?" asked Melody. "Pong needs exercise." She held up an empty plastic bag. "And you know what else he needs." She giggled.

I like dogs. But I like cats better. And that plastic bag was one reason.

"I'm going to the soccer field with Jack," I said.

"You don't play soccer," said Melody.

"I'm on a case," I said. "Or maybe I am. I haven't decided yet."

Jack came dribbling back. "Hurry," he said.

Pong jumped on the soccer ball.

"Well, I guess Pong decided," said Melody. "We're coming too."

Birds

"All right," I said. "What's the problem?"

We stood at the edge of the school soccer field.

"Birds." Jack pointed at a flock near the far goal.

"Those birds don't look like a problem to me," I said.

Just then Pong noticed the birds. He yipped and jumped like a wild thing.

Melody let Pong off his leash. He ran straight through the birds. They flew off.

"Hey," said Jack. "Pong solved my case."

"What case?" I said.

"Those birds won't leave the field. And the final game is this weekend. It's a big deal. If we win, we'll be the champions. But the birds are in the way."

"Are you nuts?" I said. "Birds won't stay on the field when teams are playing."

"Right. But they stay when I practice alone. They won't let me practice. And I need extra practice, so I can get my kick perfect. But it's all solved now. Melody, lend me Pong after school every day this week."

"Okay," said Melody. "But I have to come too."

"That's fine," said Jack. He grinned. "You don't charge anything. You're better than Sly."

Melody smiled.

Bad Mood

I left them on the field and walked toward home. This all should have been fine with me. After all, there really wasn't any case. There's no mystery to shooing birds off a field. So nothing had been solved. I shouldn't have felt bad that Jack said Melody was better than me.

Melody is my best friend. I should have been glad Jack said that dumb thing, glad because it made her feel good.

But I wasn't glad. And I didn't want to

go home and work on my drawing any-more. Jack was right. My drawing looked bad.

Besides, I'm not crazy about birds, although I had to admit Taxi was. Taxi would have loved this case. Probably any cat would.

"What's the matter with you?" Kate rode her bike in the street beside me. I wasn't surprised to see her. She lives just a couple of houses over from Jack.

"Nothing," I said.

She hopped off and walked the bike up onto the sidewalk. "Why are you frown-ing?"

"I'm not," I said.

"You're in a bad mood."

"No I'm not."

"Well, I am," said Kate. "My mother's act-ing bad."

Kate was the only person I knew who

expected her mother to do whatever she said. "What happened?" I asked.

"She said I had to go ride my bike for an hour."

"That doesn't sound bad," I said.

"I don't like riding my bike. But my mother is on a health kick with her friend Julie. She thinks exercise is wonderful. So after I finished my homework, she made me go outside."

"You already finished your homework?"

"It was easy. I traced a bird out of a magazine."

"That's cheating."

"No it's not. The teacher didn't say we couldn't trace. And don't you tell." Kate nudged me with her elbow. "Anyway, what choice did I have? It's impossible to draw good with pen. You can't erase."

"She doesn't want us to erase. That's the point."

"I know," said Kate. "She's crazy."

"She's not crazy," I said.

"Yes she is. She said we're going to draw birds all winter."

"There's nothing crazy about that," I said.

"Sure there is. Birds fly away in winter."

Ruined Grass

"Wait!" Melody was calling me.

I turned around.

Melody ran up with Pong.

"Oh, I love that puppy," said Kate. She laid her bike on the ground. Then she sat on the sidewalk and held her arms out to Pong.

Pong ran straight up Kate's front and licked her face. Kate laughed.

"I thought you were helping Jack," I said to Melody.

"He has a bad temper."

"Did he get mad at Pong?"

"He got mad at both of us. I'm never helping him again."

Pong was still licking Kate.

Kate was still laughing.

Melody laughed now too.

I thought of angry Jack, alone on the field with the birds. Sleuths have a responsibility toward their clients. Even clients who fired them before they were hired. "See you later." I walked back to the field.

Jack was jumping in the middle of the birds. He flapped his arms like a madman.

"What happened?" I called.

"That stupid dog chased the soccer ball instead of the birds."

I laughed.

"It's not funny."

"What else happened?"

"What do you mean?"

"You know. You got mad at Melody too."

"She said she could kick better than me. Then she scored on me. But only because she fouled me. Her and her stupid ballet."

"Kicking's not that important," I said.

"In soccer it is. If I don't get better at kicking, the coach will make me stay on the bench the whole game." Jack looked really worried.

I knew how he felt. I love baseball, but

I'm not that good at it. "Why don't you practice somewhere else?"

"Like where?"

"Your backyard."

"My mother says soccer ruins the lawn."

I looked out over the field. The grass was missing in lots of places. Jack's mother was right.

Jack kicked the ground. "What makes these dumb birds come here?"

That was the mystery. "We'll get rid of them," I said.

"You're hired," said Jack.

A Goal

I walked along the perimeter of the field.

Jack dribbled the ball in circles around me. "Why aren't you scaring the birds off?"

"Did they leave when you tried to scare them?"

"You know they didn't. You saw."

"Exactly," I said.

"Well, if you're not going to scare them off, how are you going to solve my problem?"

"Have you tried playing through them?"

"It doesn't work. They stay there," said Jack.

How could that be? "Let me try," I said. I kicked the ball toward the birds.

Squawk!

Oh, no!

The ball bounced off a bird and into the net.

The bird walked unsteadily. I was amazed it wasn't dead. I ran to it. It flew away. I laughed in relief.

"Wow," said Jack. "You scored. Maybe I should kick the ball into a bird."

"I didn't mean to do it," I said. "Besides,

you might hurt them. You can't play here anymore. Not till I get rid of them."

"How?"

I didn't know. But clients never like to hear that kind of answer. "Are they always out here?"

"No. They came on Monday, and they've been here every afternoon since."

"Only in the afternoon?"

"In the morning there are hardly any of them."

The Blot

Jack dribbled ahead of me. "Solve my case fast," he called. He waved and went up his walk.

By the time I got home, it was late. I helped make dinner. After we ate, I went back to my drawing.

I shaded in the wings of my bird.

Birds. So many birds all at once. Birds on the soccer field. Birds in the homework. And Kate said we would be drawing birds all winter.

But, like she said, birds fly away in winter. Not all of them, of course. But the ones that stay behind aren't easy to find.

Unless you do something to attract them.

It was November. Why were there so many birds on the soccer field?

Something was attracting them.

What would attract the birds all of a sudden? And only in the afternoon? And this late in the fall?

In thinking so hard, I pressed on the pen. The plastic near the tip broke. Ink slopped on my drawing. It formed a big blot over the bird's head.

That's exactly how I felt.

Stuart

"Why are we walking so fast?" asked Melody.

"I don't want Jack to see us."

"We can't walk fast enough not to be seen," said Melody. "We'd have to go faster than the speed of light." She giggled.

"I didn't mean it that way," I said. "I just meant if we walk fast, maybe Jack won't jump out as we go by."

"I was joking," said Melody. "You're touchy today."

The blot was still over my head. I couldn't get a grip on Jack's case.

That's how the day went. I couldn't get anything right.

In art we taped our pen drawings to the wall. Mine was almost as bad as Ben's, and Ben's was the worst.

Then Mrs. Stambaugh chose the tallest

kids to help her put up two big bird feeders outside the art room windows. That's
how she was going to attract the birds. I'm
short. I didn't get to help.

Finally, it was lunchtime. Usually I eat
with Melody. But that day I wanted to be
alone. I sat on the bleachers by the soccer
field.

A few kids were playing a pickup game.
There were hardly any birds around.

I ate my sandwich slowly. It was one of
those sunny, crisp days that makes you feel
lazy. I stretched out on a bleacher and
closed my eyes.

A whistle startled me. Everyone else had
already gone in from lunch recess. I sat up
and stared.

The whistle was coming from Stuart.
He's the school custodian. He was pushing
a green thing across the soccer field. It was
a metal funnel on wheels.

Birds fluttered down onto the field behind him.

"Hi, Stuart," I said.

"Why, hello, little miss." Stuart called all the girls "little miss" and all the boys "little sir." It didn't bother us. We knew Stuart had a tough time telling us apart. He was really nearsighted. His glasses were half an inch thick.

"What are you doing?"

"Spreading grass seed."

"In November?"

He stopped and smiled. "Most people

don't know it, but fall is a great time for planting grass. This soccer field would be bare all spring if I didn't seed it now. And you want to know the real secret?" He leaned toward me. "A little bit every day for a week, rather than a ton of seeds all at once. It works like a charm."

I looked at the seeds. They were mixed, big and little, yellow and brown, and, oh, what were those black and white ones? Aha! "You don't want flowers on the field, do you, Stuart?"

"Of course not," he said.

I knew it.

Confusion

As soon as the last bell rang, I ran outside. When Jack came out, I jumped in front of him.

"Come with me," I said.

"What are you doing jumping out at people?" said Jack. "I'm the one who jumps out at people."

"Just come."

"I have soccer practice."

"It's about your case."

Jack twisted his mouth. "Okay."

I led him to the art room.

"Well, hello, Sylvia," said Mrs. Stambaugh. "Hi, Jack."

Teachers often call me Sylvia until they get to know me better.

"Mrs. Stambaugh, can you tell us where you keep the seeds for those bird feeders?"

Mrs. Stambaugh gave us a puzzled smile. "In the shed. We can't keep them in the classroom. They might attract rodents."

"We need to go to the shed," I said.

"We already filled the feeders today," said Mrs. Stambaugh.

"There's something you need to know, though," I said.

"What?"

"Come with me. Please."

I led Mrs. Stambaugh and Jack to Stuart's shed. Sure enough, there were two giant bags inside. One held grass seed. The other held birdseed. Including big black and white ones: sunflower seeds. The birdseed one was half empty.

"Stuart switched the bags by accident," I said. "He's been seeding the soccer field with birdseed instead of grass seed."

"Oh, dear," said Mrs. Stambaugh.

"That's why there are so many birds on the field in the afternoon."

"Case solved," said Jack.

"The birds have been going to the field?" Mrs. Stambaugh brightened. "Oh, well, now even more will come to the feeder. How nice."

Sunflowers

The case of the Soccer Switch ended well. Everyone's happy again. Jack got to practice extra in time for the game, and the coach let him play a lot. Jack didn't make super kicks, but the team won anyway. So the coach was happy too. Happy enough to use team funds to buy Mrs. Stambaugh another bag of birdseed. That made Mrs. Stambaugh happy. She gave me a set of colored pencils as a reward for saving her winter project. That made Jack even happier. He said he didn't owe me anything: No one should get double payment for the same task. I gave half the pencils to Brian, so he's happy.

I can't help thinking that those birds must have missed some seeds here and there. That soccer field will look beautiful in spring, dotted with sunflowers. The thought makes me smile.

Case #2:
Sly and the Kick Craze

Determination

The school bell rang. I gathered the stuff from my cubby.

It was Tuesday. Every other day of the week, Melody and I walked home together.

But not Tuesday. On Tuesday Melody had ballet lessons. I walked home alone. Tuesday was lonely.

I went to the end of the hall and turned left onto Melody's hall out of habit. I knew she'd be gone already.

But there she was, at her cubby. She was leaning over.

"What are you doing? Aren't you late?"

"Oh, hi, Sly. I was just looking at my knees."

"You have on jeans. You can't see your knees."

"Are you in a bad mood? You get like this every Tuesday."

"Sorry." I tried to perk up. "Why were you looking at your knees?"

Melody smiled. "I was thinking about kicks."

"What about kicks?"

"You know. In ballet we do battements—high kicks with straight knees. But maybe bent knees are better underwater."

No one would see kicks underwater. I put my hand on Melody's forehead. "No fever. How come you're delirious?"

She laughed. "I just . . ."

"Hey, Melody!" Kate ran up behind Melody. "Do you have extra ballet junk I can borrow?"

Melody rolled her eyes at me. Then she turned to Kate. "It's too late. I told you. But you could start in January. That way you can ask for what you need as a Christmas present." She put on her backpack and slung her ballet bag over one shoulder.

"I want good stuff for Christmas," said Kate. "Not ballet junk."

"Stop calling it junk." Melody frowned. "The winter recital is only three weeks away. There isn't time for you to learn everything. And I don't have extra gear with me today, anyway." Melody smiled at me. "Got to go. We can talk about kicking later." She ran through the exit doors.

Kate looked at me. "I'm going to take ballet lessons." She seemed a little sad.

I knew all about Melody's recital. So I'd already figured out what they were talking about. "January is a good month to start," I said. I like to be encouraging.

"I'm starting now," said Kate. "Today."

Jack jumped out at us. "Ballet's stupid," he said. He grabbed his pack out of the cubby beside Melody's. "See ya." He waved and pushed through the exit doors. Jack likes to wave.

"Like I said," mumbled Kate, "today. My mother's going to talk to Melody's ballet teacher. My mother can talk anyone into anything." She went out the exit door.

That part about her mother was true. Kate's mother was a determined person.

If she wanted ballet lessons for Kate, she'd get them.

How much ballet could a person learn in three weeks?

Sad

I stood in my driveway and called, "Taxi."

"See?" said Brian. "She won't come."

"Taxi."

"She's cold," said Brian. "She's in a cave somewhere and she won't come out."

"Taxi doesn't get cold," I said. "She's an outdoor cat."

"It's winter," said Brian.

"Not officially. It won't be winter till December twenty-second."

"It's cold," said Brian. "I'm cold. Taxi's cold."

"Taxi's different from us. Her fur grows extra thick in the cold. It keeps her warm. Besides, she has a spot in the garage if she wants. She's happy."

"Then why won't she come?" said Brian.

He had me there. Taxi always comes when I call. She's special that way. "Taxi," I called.

Taxi appeared from the other side of the house.

I sat on the porch steps and petted her. "Where were you, Taxi? I was worried about you."

"Then take better care of her," said Brian.

I narrowed my eyes. "Who's been talking to you about cats?"

"Pets need care," said Brian.

I knew it. He'd been lectured to. "Did you do something bad to Wilson?"

Brian blinked. "It was an accident."

"What did you do?"

"Well, not an accident. A mistake."

"What did you do?"

"Frogs like water," said Brian. "And a shower is water."

"You gave Wilson a shower?" I imagined a bunch of frogs in Brian's bathtub. Then I imagined his mother discovering them. I put my hand over my mouth so Brian couldn't see my grin. After all, it's not nice to laugh at someone's mother. "That doesn't sound like such a bad mistake."

"The shampoo got Wilson sick," said Brian.

"Shampoo? Brian, frogs don't even have hair."

Brian picked up a clump of dirt and

smashed it on the driveway. "Wilson better get strong again." He didn't look at me, but I could see his chin crumple.

I went over to Brian. I put my arms around him. "I hope so, Brian."

"Is he crying?" Melody came through Brian's yard. Her backyard touched his, so we always cut through his. "Come hug me, Brian. We can cry together." Her face was so sad.

Brian looked at her. "Did your puppy die?"

"No," said Melody. "Why would you ask such a terrible thing?"

"He's just worried about Wilson," I said.
"What happened, Melody?"

"My recital's ruined."

Jumping to Conclusions

"The recital will be wonderful even if Kate's in it," I said.

"What?" said Melody.

"Kate won't be good, but who cares? You can still do everything perfectly. And when Kate messes up, you'll look even better."

"What are you talking about?" said Melody.

"Kate. Her mother got her into your ballet class, right?"

Melody shook her head. "What gave you that idea?"

This was embarrassing. I had jumped to conclusions. My father says a good sleuth never jumps to conclusions. "Tell me what you're talking about," I said in a business-like voice.

Melody reached into the pocket of her jacket and pulled out a pair of ballet slippers. "Smell."

I stepped back. "I don't want to smell your shoes."

"No one should. They stink. They're my old pair. Pong ruined them before he was trained, if you know what I mean." Melody giggled. But the next moment her eyes filled with tears. "My good pair disappeared. And they cost a lot. My mother won't buy me a new pair till she's convinced they're really gone." Melody sniffled.

I thought about the time I lost my baseball glove. "Maybe they're in your closet under something."

"You're the messy one," said Melody. "Nothing gets lost in my closet."

"Maybe Pong took them."

"I looked everywhere."

"Maybe . . ."

"Everywhere, Sly. I'm careful."

"I believe you."

"They were stolen. And I'm hiring you to get them back."

Taxi didn't care one bit about ballet. I didn't either. "I've never taken a criminal case before."

"Please." Melody sniffled again. "My mother says my old slippers will have to do for now. But they stink. My good ones smell sweet."

"I have sweet shoes. And sweet feet." Brian pulled at his shoelaces. "Sweet teeth too." By now his shoeslaces were a tangled mess. "My mother says it's a problem. Fix my shoes."

I sat on the ground and worked on unknotting Brian's shoelaces. "That's not really true," I said to Melody.

"What?"

"Your good slippers smell like old sweaters in the rain."

"That's lanolin," said Melody. "I rub them with lanolin to keep them soft."

"Well, lanolin stinks."

"That's your opinion. I like it." Melody sighed. She could be very dramatic. "At lesson today Mrs. Munson made me sit on the bench. She gave me an ice pack."

"Why would she give you an ice pack for wearing old slippers?"

"I didn't wear my old slippers. I didn't know my good ones were stolen till I got to ballet lesson and they weren't in my bag. I had to dance just in tights. And I stubbed my toe. I hate ice packs."

"Oh," I said, finally working Brian's shoelaces free. "That's awful."

"Ice packs burn," said Brian. He took off his loose shoe and ripped off his sock. He stuck his foot in my face. "Smell."

"I don't smell feet. It's too cold to go barefoot, Brian. Put your shoe back on." I stood up. "How can an ice pack burn?"

"It's true," said Melody. "They're so cold, they burn."

"They have jelly inside," said Brian.

"How . . ." began Melody.

But I shook my head no at her. If we gave Brian any excuse, he'd talk nonstop.

"Does your toe still hurt?"

"A little."

"Soak it in hot water with salt."

"Why?" asked Melody.

My mother soaked her feet in salt whenever they gave her problems. But sleuths don't use their mothers as a reason. It makes clients lose confidence. "It works."

"All right. But that's not the problem."

"I know. The problem is finding who stole your slippers."

"And getting them back," said Melody. "I don't want to dance in the recital in my old stinky ones."

"No one in the audience will be able to smell them," I said.

"I'll smell them. Will you take my case?"

I like mysteries, not crimes. "I'm not sure."

The Phone Call

"Let's make a phone call."

We went inside. Brian came too. "Taxi's cold," he said to my mother.

"I'm sorry to hear that," said Mother. She wiped her hands on a dish towel. "Want to come have a snack and tell me about it?"

Brian sat at the kitchen table.

Melody and I went into the living room. I picked up the telephone and dialed.

"Hello."

"Hello, Kate. I have a question for you. Did you ask for ballet slippers for Christmas?"

"No," said Kate.

"Did your mother buy you ballet slippers already?"

"No," said Kate.

"Did you dance without slippers in today's ballet class?"

"No," said Kate.

Aha! "Did you take Melody's ballet slippers?"

"No," said Kate. "That's four questions. Now it's my turn. Are you completely nuts?"

"No," I said.

"Why did you ask me those crazy questions about slippers? I'm not even taking ballet."

"Why aren't you taking ballet?" I asked.

"I asked first," said Kate.

"Somebody stole Melody's ballet slippers," I said.

"Oh. Well, I'm not taking ballet because I don't want to. It was my mother's idea in the first place."

"You said your mother could talk anyone into anything," I said.

"She can," said Kate.

56

"She didn't talk you into ballet," I said.

"You're right. But she talked me into exercise. She's still on that health kick. So I figured out I want to be a cheerleader instead. And that's what I'm going to do." Kate hung up.

I looked at Melody. "Kate didn't steal them."

"Don't worry," said Melody. "You'll find the criminal. I have faith in you."

Lost and Found

Melody came into the lunchroom wearing her backpack.

"Why are you wearing your backpack?"

"So I could show you." She grinned. "Look." She took off her backpack and unzipped the outer pocket.

I peeked. "Your slippers!"

"They were in my cubby this morning when I got to school. They must have fallen out of my ballet bag yesterday and I didn't notice."

"That's terrific. Your recital is saved."

"And the case is solved." Melody patted her slippers lovingly. Then she zipped the pocket and put her pack on again. "What do I owe you?"

"I never took the case." Besides, I didn't solve it. I'd made one of the worst mistakes a sleuth can make. I had assumed something without proof. The slippers weren't stolen. Maybe I was slipping as a sleuth.

I took a bite of my apple and tried to pep myself up. "Let's celebrate when we get home today. We can make milk shakes."

"I can't. I'm staying after school."

"What for?"

"I have swim team practice," said Melody.

"Swim team?" I put down my apple. "Since when?"

"Two weeks ago."

"You joined the team two whole weeks ago and you never told me?"

"I've been meaning to tell you." Melody shrugged. "But every time I start, we get interrupted."

"Wow." The things you don't know about people.

I really was slipping.

"Don't look so sad," said Melody. "It's not like I was keeping it a secret or anything."

"But I should have noticed," I said.

"How? Last Wednesday you had a dentist appointment. And that was the first meeting of the team."

"Oh." I felt better. Good old Melody. I

picked up my apple again and chewed slowly. "I thought you hated swimming."

"I do. I always feel like I'm drowning. We start with fifteen minutes of kickboard time. The coach clocks us. I'm bad at it, no matter how hard I kick."

"What's that?" Jack sat down across from us. "Did you say something about being bad at kicking?"

Melody stiffened. "It's not nice to eavesdrop."

"What did she say?" Jack said to me.

"You have to ask her," I said.

"What did you say?" Jack said to Melody.

"I have to go." Melody got up. "See you later, Sly." She left. And she hadn't even eaten her sandwich.

"What's wrong with her?" asked Jack.

"She joined the swim team."

"The swim team. That's a real sport. Not like stupid ballet."

I didn't like ballet. But I was Melody's best friend. I pointed my carrot at Jack. "Ballet's just as athletic as any sport."

Jack took my carrot. "Thanks. So what was she saying about kicking bad?"

"She doesn't kick bad. She kicks good. She's just bad at the kickboard. Her swim coach drills her."

"He drills her at kicking?"

"I guess."

Jack stuffed his sandwich in his mouth and got up. He left. He didn't even say good-bye.

First Melody. Now Jack.

I felt like I had cooties.

The Cooler

I walked home alone. When I got to Melody's house, I cut through Brian's yard.

Brian came bursting out his back door. He ran into my garage. He carried out a picnic cooler. "Get a knife."

I decided to ignore that. He was four, and four-year-olds know they're not supposed to play with knives. "Whose cooler is that?"

"My mother threw it out." He set it in the driveway and took the top off. Then he brushed the inside with his hands and put the top back on. "Get a knife."

"How did it get in my garage?"

"I put it there."

"Why?" I asked.

"It's Taxi's new home. Get a knife."

"Brian, a cat can't sleep in a picnic cooler."

"It'll keep her warm," said Brian.

"She'd suffocate."

Brian turned the cooler upside down and pointed. "Cut a door."

I thought about it. Picnic coolers were

insulated. They should keep in heat as eas-
ily as they kept in cold. It was ridiculous,
but Brian was right. With a door in the
side, the cooler would be like an igloo.
Taxi might like it. She might like it better
than her wooden box with the blanket in
the garage. "Wait here." I went inside and
got the old bread knife Dad used for helping me on projects.

My mother was chopping carrots.
"Where are you going with that knife, Sly?"

"To cut a hole in a picnic cooler."

"Why on earth would you want to do a
thing like that?"

"Sly," called Melody. She stood at the porch door.

"I thought you were at swim team practice."

"I was. Oh, Sly, everything is ruined."

I put down the knife. "Come on in, Melody."

Fins

We went upstairs to my bedroom to talk in private.

As soon as I shut the door, Melody paced. "I'll never get good at the dumb kickboard now. And I'll never feel comfortable in the water. And they won't pick me. And my whole spring's ruined."

"Sit down."

Melody sat on the edge of my bed.

"Take a deep breath."

Melody took a deep breath.

"Do you know that you use the word 'ruin' at least once a day? You're dramatic, Melody."

"Do you really think so?" Melody said hopefully. "Really?"

This was going nowhere. "You're already on the team. They take everyone who comes. So you don't have to worry about getting picked."

"That's not what I meant." Melody bit the side of her thumbnail.

"Okay, tell me what's wrong."

"It happened again."

"What happened again?"

"My fins disappeared."

"You don't have fins."

"Yes I do. Everyone on the swim team has fins."

Oh, that kind of fins. "I was joking," I said.

"Really?"

"No. So where were these fins?"

"In my cubby. They were stolen."

"You mean like the last time?" I said.

"Don't make fun of me," said Melody. "I didn't make fun of you when you thought I meant real fins."

"Sorry. Let me get this straight. You had fins in your cubby?"

"Yes," said Melody. "And this time there is definitely a thief. I checked my cubby. Fins are big. You can't miss them."

"This is weird," I said.

"So will you take my case?"

Taxi loved fish, and fish had fins. Taxi would love this case. Probably any cat would. "Yes," I said.

"Good." Melody got up.

"Wait. Tell me what you meant before. About getting picked and spring."

"It's kind of a long story. And, anyway, it's not that big a deal. I was just being dramatic. Like you said. I've got to go now."

Melody had been my best friend for as long as I could remember. I knew things about her. Right now I knew she was keeping a secret. From me.

Brilliant

I followed Melody downstairs.

We went out to the driveway.

My mother was on her knees beside Brian. They were putting duct tape over the rough edges of a freshly cut door in the side of the cooler. "Come see," Mother said. "It's a little house for Taxi to sleep in outside."

"I know," I said.

"It's cute," Melody said.

"It's Brian's invention. Isn't it brilliant?" Mother's voice was proud. You'd think Brian was her child.

My cheeks got hot, even out here in the

chilly air. It wasn't nice to be jealous of a four-year-old. I smiled as big as I could. "It's great, Brian." I turned to Melody. "Are you sure you have to go so fast?"

"I need to do something."

"Can I help?"

Melody blinked at me. "Maybe."

We cut through Brian's yard and Pong jumped on us. He was tied to a long rope, so he could run all over Melody's yard.

"Do they make coolers big enough for dogs?" asked Melody.

"Pong sleeps inside at night," I said grumpily. "And he's got a doghouse for the day."

"Yeah, but a doghouse isn't as interesting as a cooler. You think I could find one big enough for him?"

"I don't know," I said even more grumpily. "What do you need help with?"

"Don't make fun of me."

"I won't."

Melody lay down in the grass on her stomach. She held out her arms in front. "Pull me."

"Pull you?"

"I didn't get my full kickboard workout because I didn't have my fins. So I need extra practice. Pull."

"I don't understand."

"Just pull. And I'll kick. It'll be like I'm in the pool."

This was the wackiest idea I'd ever heard from Melody. "Have you been talking to Brian?"

Melody sat up in a huff. "You said you wouldn't make fun."

"Melody, this makes no sense."

"Yes it does. Coach said it was good to have people pull us while we kick."

"He meant in a pool."

"Well, I don't have a pool," said Melody. "I have grass."

"There's too much friction."

Melody went over to her garbage can. She took out a big cardboard box. She flattened it. Then she lay down on it and held out her arms. "Either pull or go home."

I pulled.

Spring

Thursday at lunch Melody came in wearing her backpack again.

She sat down beside me. "You're not going to believe what I found in my cubby."

"Really?" I said.

She took off the backpack and unzipped the big compartment.

Two long red fins were stuffed inside. "They're pretty," I said.

"They were there when I got to school."

"Strange," I said.

"Do you think I'm losing my mind?"

I thought about pulling Melody through the grass the day before. I swallowed. "Not really."

"What do I owe you?"

"It wasn't a real case," I said. "Don't pay me."

"All right," said Melody. "But I'll give you two baseball cards, as a present then."

Melody didn't play baseball, but she collected the cards.

"Thanks."

Jack plopped down across from us. "What are you talking about?"

"It's private," said Melody. "Don't you usually eat with the guys?"

"They don't give me carrots," said Jack. Melody looked at me.

"I didn't actually give him carrots," I said. "I pointed one at him and he took it."

"So, anyway, how's the swimming?" asked Jack.

Melody looked at me again.

"I guess it sort of slipped out," I said.

"Not a good enough kicker for it, huh?" said Jack. "Your coach giving you a hard time?"

"Hey, be nice," said Melody, "or I'll go out for soccer and kick your you-know-what."

Jack's mouth dropped open. "You're going to go out for the spring league?"

"Who knows what I'll do in spring? I might do anything." Melody got up. "See you later, Sly. We can practice in the grass after school."

She left. Without eating.

And what was all this talk about spring? Yesterday she said spring would be ruined without her swim fins. And now she said she might do anything in spring.

Jack got up.

"Don't you dare leave me sitting here alone," I said.

Jack left.

I really did have cooties.

Way to give a girl a complex.

I lost my appetite.

Generosity

After school, Melody went home to eat. She said she was starving because she'd skipped lunch.

I said I was hungry too. I don't use words like "starving." I'm not dramatic. But she didn't invite me in.

I went home with two new baseball cards. Taxi's cooler sat by the porch step. I peeked inside. No Taxi.

Brian came out of his house. "Wilson got better," he said.

"That's great, Brian."

"Is Taxi in her cooler?"

Taxi had refused to go in the cooler. She hated it. Secretly, this made me a little bit glad. "No, Brian. Sorry."

"Want a cookie?"

"Did your mom make them?" Brian's mom made the worst cookies. Whole wheat, sunflower seeds, and who knew what else. Brian's mom was a health food nut. Maybe he was offering just to get rid of them.

"I helped her. I rolled the dough. With a big rolling pin. It's heavy."

I was hungry. But not that hungry. "No sweets before dinner."

"You can take one for later," said Brian. He reached into his pocket and pulled out a thick cookie. It looked like a dog biscuit

"Oh, hey," I said quickly. "Here comes Melody."

Melody crossed Brian's yard. She carried a half sandwich in each hand.

"Want a cookie?" Brian said to Melody.

Melody gave me a knowing look. "Uh, not now, Brian."

Brian's eyes got sad. I think he was being genuinely generous.

"I brought sandwiches for you and Sly. Tuna." She held them out. She was being generous too.

I took a bite of my half sandwich. And suddenly I got into the spirit of generosity. "Taxi," I called.

Taxi came running.

I put a piece of sandwich in Taxi's cooler and shoved the cooler in Taxi's path.

She went right inside.

"Yay!" screamed Brian. He threw the cookie into the air and ran around us. "Taxi loves her cooler!"

Melody peeked into the cooler. "She sure likes tuna."

"It's her favorite," I said.

"Taxi tuna, tuna Taxi," screamed Brian. He threw his half sandwich into the cooler.

"I'm glad you came over." I finished eating. "Thanks for the food."

"Ready to pull me?"

"No. I'm ready to talk," I said.

"I knew this was coming," said Melody.

"Why did you join the swim team when you hate swimming?"

"I need to get comfortable in the water."

"Why?" I asked.

Melody looked away.

"I'm your best friend, Melody."

"All right, but you can't tell."

"I'd never tell your secrets," I said.

"I won't either," said Brian.

"You told Jack about the swim team."

"That was a mistake," I said.

"I never talk to Jack," said Brian. "Or just sometimes. Just Saturdays. I only talk to Jack on Saturdays. And sometimes Tuesdays. And June. Sometimes June."

Brian loves June. His birthday is in June.

"I know it has to do with spring," I said. "So just tell."

"The school spring play is going to be *The Little Mermaid.*"

"I love the little mermaid," said Brian.

"Everyone loves her," said Melody.

And I got it. "That's what you meant about getting picked. You want the part."

"You have no idea how hard it is to move

a kickboard fast, Sly. I kick like a maniac, and all I do is make bubbles and get tired."

"What's the kickboard got to do with the play?"

"I want to be a good mermaid. But you can't tell anyone, because they might join the swim team too, and get better than me."

This was way too dumb for Melody. Maybe she really had lost her mind. "Melody, mermaids don't kick," I said softly. "They don't have legs."

Melody's eyes teared up. "Well, I know that."

"And the play will be on the stage. The water will just be a blue sheet or something."

Melody's bottom lip quivered. "I know that too. But the swim team coach is the drama teacher. And he believes in method acting."

"What's that?" asked Brian.

Exactly my question.

"It's where actors try to really experience something, so they can act better."

"How's that acting then? I mean, if you experience it, you're not acting."

"Don't argue with me, Sly. It's not my idea. I just thought that if the coach saw me swimming good, he'd think I was a natural for the part."

"You are a natural for the part."

"You're just saying that because you're my best friend."

"I'm saying it because you're so dramatic."

"Really?"

"You'd be better if you had a fish tail," said Brian.

"The costume will have a fish tail," said Melody.

"Good." Brian jumped in a circle. "I want a fish tail too."

"If I get the part, I'll let you wear it sometimes."

"Yay."

"Now you can quit the swim team," I said. "Let's celebrate."

"I'll go get more cookies," said Brian.

Cleats

On Friday Melody came into the lunchroom with her backpack on again.

I stared. "What now?"

"Soccer shoes." Melody put her backpack on the bench beside her. "Beat-up ones. They smell."

"Well, at least this proves you aren't losing your mind," I said.

"Who would put smelly old soccer shoes in my cubby?"

Disappearing ballet slippers. Disappearing swim fins. And now magically appearing soccer shoes.

They all had to do with feet.

"Who cares about your feet, Melody? Besides you, I mean."

"My daddy does. He tickles them."

"Other than him?"

"No one."

"Let's be logical about this. Someone took away your ballet slippers, so you couldn't have a good lesson."

Melody nodded.

"And someone took away your swim fins, so you couldn't have a good practice."

Melody nodded.

"Someone doesn't want you dancing or swimming. But someone wants you playing soccer."

"I don't like soccer," said Melody. "I'll just throw them away."

She opened her pack and I saw the shoes inside.

"Those aren't for soccer. The spikes are

metal. Those are for baseball." I turned a cleat over. Written in red crayon on the bottom was the number 2. I recognized red crayon numbers. "Eat, Melody. And when Jack sits down with us, don't leave, no matter what he says."

"What makes you so sure Jack will sit with us again?"

Just then Kate came over. She looked me up and down. "It doesn't matter if you're short."

"What are you talking about?"

"Cheerleading. You can do it," said Kate. Jack jumped out at all of us.

"You're good at jumping," said Kate. "You'd make a good cheerleader."

"I'm a guy," said Jack.

"Guys can be cheerleaders," said Kate. "I'm putting together a squad. We're going to jump high."

"You better not jump higher than me,"

said Jack. "I'm tired of people doing things better than me."

Suddenly a memory came. A while back Melody had told Jack she kicked better than him. That cinched it. "What else did you get at Goodwill yesterday, Jack?"

"How did you know I was there?"

"Join the cheerleading squad," said Kate. She can be very persistent.

"You bought these." I put the smelly baseball cleats on the table.

"That's disgusting," said Kate. She left.

"You're the one who took Melody's ballet slippers."

"I gave them back," said Jack.

"And you took her swim fins."

"I gave them back too," said Jack.

"And you left these cleats in her cubby."

"And they smell," said Melody.

"There's no rule against that," said Jack.

"There is a rule against stealing," said Melody.

"It's not stealing if you give it back," said Jack. "It's a prank."

I pointed to the red crayon number. "You paid two dollars. And you never have extra money. Why was it so important to mess up Melody's ballet lesson?"

"I didn't really mess it up. My cousin told me."

"What did your cousin say?" said Melody.

"That you're the best in the class."

"Really?" said Melody. She smiled shyly at Jack.

She was supposed to be mad at him.

"You messed up her swimming practice," I said firmly.

Jack looked ashamed.

"I hate swimming anyway," said Melody.

Jack looked surprised.

Melody smiled again. "Why'd you give me those shoes?"

"Ask Sly," said Jack. "She thinks she has it all figured out."

"He wanted you to go out for baseball. That way you wouldn't go out for the spring soccer league. You can't do two sports at once."

"I'm not going out for soccer," said Melody.

"Really?" said Jack.

"I never even thought about it," said Melody. "Not really."

They were so chummy, it made me sick.

This time I was the one to leave them sitting in the lunchroom.

Good Feelings

Jack really was sorry that his pranks got out of hand. And Melody was sorry she'd hurt Jack's feelings. She told me all about how they apologized to each other.

Melody promised never to brag about her kicks again. But Jack decided to do extra work on his kicks anyway. He joined the swim team.

The ballet recital was this evening. Melody was terrific. I told her that. So did Jack. He came because his cousin was in it.

Kate complimented Melody too. She came because she was scouting for people for her cheerleading squad. She went around telling the best dancers to "join us." When I asked her who "us" was, she admitted it was just her so far. Poor Kate. If I liked that sort of thing, I'd have joined just to keep her company. It's okay, though, because Melody finally joined.

The case of the Kick Craze is over. And even though Melody had already paid in advance, with those two baseball cards, she gave me a bottle of nail polish too.

So I'm going to bed happy tonight. But first I'm going outside to say good night to Taxi. She's in her cooler, snug and warm, with one paw hanging out the door. This afternoon I told Brian my mother was right—the cooler was a brilliant idea. He beamed. Jealousy is nasty. Good riddance.

Yup, I sure am going to bed happy tonight.

Case #3:

Sly and the Basketball Blues

The Captain

The cheerleading squad met after school.

On Monday we met at Kate's house. That's because the whole idea of the squad was Kate's.

We skipped Tuesday because Melody has ballet lessons on Tuesday.

On Wednesday we met at Melody's house. That's because Melody was the first person besides Kate to join the squad. Kate had promised Melody that Pong could be mascot if she joined.

On Thursday we met at Princess's house. That's because Princess was the next to join Kate's squad. She's new in school. Anyone can push her around. Especially with a name like Princess. Her father gave her that nickname and it stuck. Poor kid. Her big sister is called Angel. It's a good thing there aren't any more girls in the family.

On Friday we met at my house. I didn't want to be on the cheerleading squad. I hated the whole idea. But Melody is my best friend. And when Kate roped Melody into it, Melody begged me to join too.

My latest case began that first Friday, in our driveway. I didn't know it was beginning, though. Here's how it went.

"Line up," said Kate.

Melody and Princess lined up. Brian lined up too. I didn't line up.

"Line up," said Kate, looking at me.

"It's my house," I said. "I'll do what I want."

"I'm the captain," said Kate. "You'll do what I say."

"She's the captain," said Brian. "Oh, my. Hurry, Sly."

"She's only the captain of the cheerleading squad," I told Brian. "She can't hurt us." But I got in line anyway.

"You," said Kate, pointing at Brian. "Get out of line. You can't be a cheerleader."

Too Little

Brian cried.

I put my arm around his shoulders. "Why can't he be a cheerleader?"

"He's too little," said Kate.

"It doesn't matter if you're short." I pulled Brian closer. "You said so yourself."

"It does if you're that short."

"We could carry him," said Melody.

"Yeah," said Brian.

"How can we cheerlead if we're carrying him?" said Kate.

"Not in our arms," said Melody. "On our backs. We can take turns."

This was a bad idea. Brian is heavy. But Melody was just trying to be nice. And it's important to stand up to Kate. "Okay, Brian." I got down on one knee. "Climb on my back."

Brian climbed on. He clamped his legs

around my waist. He locked his arms around my throat. I couldn't breathe.

"You're turning purple," said Princess.

"Let go, Brian," said Melody. "You're strangling Sly."

"Oh, no." Brian let go. He fell off me.

"See," said Kate. "You can't cheerlead."

Brian rubbed his elbow. He hurt it when he fell off me. He moved close to me and looked hard at Kate.

I looked hard at Kate.

Melody looked hard at Kate.

Even Princess looked hard at Kate.

"Stop it, all of you," said Kate. "Listen, Brian, you can clap for us, okay? Cheerleaders need an audience to clap for them."

cheering

"Jump higher," said Kate.

"Shout louder," said Kate.

"Kick harder," said Kate.

Melody and Princess and I jumped and shouted and kicked.

Brian clapped.

This was no fun at all. I sat on the ground. "What are we cheering for anyway?" I asked. "Our school doesn't have a football team."

"We could cheer for track," said Princess.

"No one cheers for track," I said.

"We could cheer for baseball," said Melody. "You love baseball."

"No one cheers for baseball," I said. "And when baseball season starts, I'll be playing, not cheering. Playing is a lot more fun than cheering."

"It is?" asked Brian.

"Of course," I said.

"Basketball," said Kate. "I already decided. Last night."

"Our school doesn't play other schools in basketball," I said.

"But they play against themselves," said Kate. "So we'll cheer for both sides."

"That's nice," said Princess.

"Have you ever played a team sport, Princess?" I asked.

"No."

I knew it. "We can't cheer for both sides at once," I said. "It won't work."

Kate put her hands on her hips and stood over me. "Don't be so negative, Sly."

Just then Kate's mother came jogging up the sidewalk. She held a giant bag in her arms.

"Why's your mother here?" I asked.

"She brought us something." Kate ran to meet her. Her mother jogged in place while Kate took the bag. Then she waved and jogged away.

Kate's mother was still on her health kick.

Brian poked at the bag. "What's in it?"

"Props."

Props

"Pom-poms!" Kate handed them out.

"Cool," said Melody.

"Cool," said Princess.

I had to admit, those pom-poms were cool.

"I want pom-poms," said Brian.

Kate reached around in the bottom of the bag. "Good. My mother remembered the measuring tape." She handed me a coiled cloth tape. "Climb that tree, Sly."

"I want pom-poms," said Brian.

"The maple tree? Why?" I asked.

"We have to put up a basketball hoop."

"I want pom-poms," said Brian.

"You can't put a basketball hoop on a tree," I said.

"We're not using it to really play," said Kate. "It's just to give us the right atmosphere. My mother bought us four kiddie hoops." She held out a plastic hoop. "We can put one up at each of our houses. Then when we practice, we can pretend the team just made a basket."

"I want pom-poms," said Brian.

This reminded me of Melody's method acting. "We can pretend the team just made a basket without putting up kiddie hoops," I said.

"The hoops will make us cheer more realistically," said Kate.

"What's realistic about cheering?" I asked.

"Are you afraid of climbing the tree?" asked Kate.

"I wouldn't say that," I said. "I just don't like climbing trees."

"I want pom-poms," said Brian.

"I climb trees," said Princess. In a flash, she was halfway up the maple.

Taxi came jumping out of the tree.

Brian went over and petted her.

"How high should I go?" Princess called down.

"Catch," said Kate. She threw the tape. It hit the trunk and fell in the dirt.

"I'll throw it," I said. "I'm the one who plays baseball, after all." I threw Princess the tape.

"Now, hold on to one end and let the other fall loose," said Kate. "The hoop has to go ten feet up."

Princess let one end of the tape dangle down.

"Climb higher," said Kate.

Princess went higher.

"Stop," called Kate. "Oh, dear. You should have taken the hoop with you."

"I'll hand it to her," said Melody. She climbed the tree and handed Princess the hoop.

"You're not a squad of cheerleaders; you're more like a troop of monkeys," I said.

"Don't be a bad sport," said Kate.

"I want pom-poms," said Brian. He petted Taxi behind the ears.

High

Brian and I stood under the maple looking up. The others had gone home.

The hoop was finally in place. It stuck out at a weird angle.

"What's it for?" asked Brian.

"The hoop? Haven't you ever seen a basketball game, Brian?"

"No. What's it for?"

"Players throw balls into it."

Brian picked up a rock. He threw it. It didn't even hit the lowest branch.

"You have to be tall to play basketball," I said.

"Can you throw a ball that high?"

"Sometimes. We play in the gym at school. It's hard, though."

"Brian," called Brian's mother from their kitchen door.

Brian went home.

I rubbed my hands in the dirt. It was cold, and the dirt was hard. But I knew dirt keeps hands from slipping. So I rubbed till I had a good layer.

I climbed that maple tree. Not all the way to the hoop. But high enough.

I don't like heights.

But I refuse to be the only chicken cheerleader.

Prunes

On Saturday afternoon, Melody and I made beads out of clay. A few minutes after she went home, there was a knock on the porch door.

I hadn't had a job sleuthing for a while, and I missed it. So I tried to guess who was at the door. Just to oil up my skills.

It wasn't Jack. Jack doesn't knock. He kicks his soccer ball at the door.

It wasn't Kate. Kate went to visit her uncle's farm this weekend.

It wasn't Brian. He comes in without knocking.

Maybe it was Princess. She's a little shy, though. She'd call before coming over.

I opened the door.

"Oh, good, Sly, you're home." It was Brian's mother. She was holding a plate of cookies. They looked dreadful.

"What's up, Mrs. Olsen? Do you want to come in?"

She looked back over her shoulder. Then she looked at me again. "No. Brian's playing in the backyard alone, and he doesn't know I'm over here. So I mustn't stay. I just wanted to talk to you for a minute."

"Sure." I waited.

"You haven't spent much time with Brian lately."

"I've been busy."

"Is that it?" Mrs. Olsen lowered her eyebrows a little. She looked sort of like a chimp. "Or did Brian do something to upset you?"

"Oh, no. Brian didn't do anything. I have cheerleading," I said. "We practice after school at different houses. So I'm only home on Tuesday and Friday now."

"Ah. So Brian hasn't done anything strange around you?"

"Has he done something strange around you?" I asked.

"This morning he had a friend over. Little Mitchell, from his nursery school. And Brian snuck into the kitchen and got my marble rolling pin, the one we made these cookies with—they're for you, by the way." She handed me the plate.

I smiled bravely. "Thank you."

"They've got prunes in them."

Prunes in cookies. "Thank you."

"Anyway, Brian made Mitchell roll him."

"Roll him?"

"Yes. As though he was dough. He made Mitchell roll his legs and arms and chest."

"That is a little strange," I said.

"And it hurt. Brian kept saying, 'Ouch,' and Mitchell wanted to stop, and Brian wouldn't let him, and then Mitchell came and got me."

"Oh," I said. "I guess that's stranger than I thought."

"And he won't tell me why. So I was wondering if you'd talk to him." Mrs. Olsen smiled. "You seem to understand him better than anyone."

"Sure."

What Works

Mrs. Olsen went into her house.

I went into her backyard. Brian was perched in the lowest crook of their apple tree.

He smiled at me as I came over. "Watch." He put his hands on a branch and hung for about a tenth of a second. He dropped to the ground onto his bottom. "Ouch."

"Brian, what's that you've got around your ankles?"

"I hung," said Brian.

"I saw." I waited for him to answer my question.

"You climbed your tree yesterday," said Brian.

I didn't know anyone had seen me. "I was just experimenting," I said. I knelt beside him. "You've got a duct tape roll around your ankle."

"I had to push to get it on," said Brian. "I had to squash my foot. Squish squash."

"Is that our duct tape roll?"

"I'm going to give it back," said Brian. He pulled on it. "Help me."

I eased Brian's foot out. The duct tape roll was pretty heavy. "This is a bad thing to do, Brian. Look, it made a red mark across the top of your foot."

Brian rubbed his foot.

"That must hurt," I said.

Brian stopped rubbing his foot. He just looked at me.

"And you've got a magnet held on with a rubber band on your other ankle."

Brian smiled. "Magnets work." He reached over and picked up another magnet from the ground under the tree.

"Work at what? What do magnets do?"

"Don't you know? I thought you were smart, Sly."

I sat on the ground beside him. "Why did you make Mitchell roll you with the rolling pin?"

"It didn't work," said Brian.

"Were you trying to make it work? Did you want to become a cookie?"

Brian laughed. "You're funny, Sly. Maybe you're dumb. But I love you anyway."

"Listen, Brian, your mother is worried about you. So stop doing strange things."

"My mother is worried?" Brian looked somber. "Make me a list."

"What kind of a list?"

"A list of strange things."

He had a point.

Dinner

"First, no more having people roll you with the rolling pin."

"It didn't work anyway," said Brian.

"Second, no more wearing duct tape rolls and magnets on your ankles."

Brian looked away.

At least he wasn't a liar. He wouldn't make a promise he had no intention of keeping.

"Want to tell me why you're doing these strange things?" I asked.

"Brian," called his mother from the kitchen door. "Do you want humus for dinner? Or tofu?"

"Raisins," said Brian.

His mother shut the door.

"What's humus?" I asked.

"Yellow mush."

"What's tofu?"

"White stuff. It jiggles."

"Raisins are a good choice," I said.

He nodded.

I thought about Brian's dinner. "Want to eat with us tonight? We're having chicken and rice."

"Okay."

So I asked Mrs. Olsen and she agreed.

It was my job to make the rice. I'm good at it. I let Brian help me measure. "Two cups," I said. "That's plenty."

Brian looked in the pot with dismay. "That's nothing. We're going to be hungry."

"No we won't. We'll add water and boil it, and it will fill the pot."

"Really?"

"Sure, water makes it swell."

"Good," said Brian.

Hired

The phone rang early Sunday morning. It was for me.

"Sly, this is Mrs. Olsen."

"Good morning, Mrs. Olsen."

"I want to hire you—as Sly the Sleuth."

"Is it about Brian? About how strange he's acting?"

"Yes," said Mrs. Olsen.

Taxi loved Brian. Brian was good to her. He had made her a picnic cooler to sleep in. So Taxi would care about this case. Probably any cat would.

Plus, I loved Brian too. "I accept the job," I said.

"How much money do you charge for being a sleuth?"

No adult had ever asked me that before. All my past clients had been kids. They paid me with objects, not money. I felt silly to name a price. And I had no idea what the price should be. "For you, noth-ing," I said, wondering if I should have asked for ten dollars.

"Then I'll pay you in cookies," said Mrs. Olsen.

I should have asked for ten dollars. "That's not necessary," I said.

"Oh, I love to bake, don't worry about that."

"Let's count yesterday's cookies as payment," I said.

She laughed. "That's only the first installment."

I gave up. "We might as well get started. Has Brian done anything else strange?"

"That's why I'm calling so early. He's in the bathtub."

I'd given Brian a bath before. He made his rubber shark eat his rubber ducklings. Then he made his rubber ducklings gang up against the shark and eat it. He loved baths. "Taking a bath isn't strange," I said.

"He's been in there for an hour. He says he's not getting out till it works."

That's what Brian had talked about Saturday—something working. "Till what works?" I asked.

"I have no idea," said Mrs. Olsen. "He won't give me a straight answer. But he's really sad. That's why I hired you."

The Blues

I knocked on the bathroom door. "Want to get out of the tub, Brian?"

"Not till it works."

"Can I come in?"

"Yes."

I went in and closed the toilet seat cover and sat on it. Brian was underwater except for the oval of his eyes and nose and mouth.

"What's supposed to work?"

"The water."

I made a show of examining him. "It's working," I said.

"Really?" Brian sat up. He inspected his arms and legs. "No it's not."

"You look pretty clean to me," I said.

Brian plopped back under the water. "It better work," he said. "Nothing else did."

"Okay, Brian, let's figure this out. The rolling pin didn't work," I said slowly.

"Nope."

"Did you try duct tape again?"

"We had a roll too."

"And it didn't work?"

"Nope."

"And the water isn't working."

"You forgot the magnet," said Brian.

"Oh, yeah, the magnet didn't work?"

"Nope," said Brian.

What did a rolling pin and duct tape and a magnet and water all have in common?

"You better get out, Brian," I said. "Your hands are wrinkling from the water."

"Oh, no," said Brian. "It's working just the opposite." He cried.

"You sure have the blues, Brian. What do you mean, it's working the opposite."

"I'm shrinking, not swelling."

And it suddenly made sense. "Rice," I said.

Fun

I helped Brian towel off.

"First, you're not shrinking."

"Really?"

"Really. Now let me get this straight. You wanted the water to make you bigger. To swell you, like rice."

"It didn't work."

"And you wanted the rolling pin to make you bigger like cookie dough."

"It didn't work either," said Brian. "And it hurt. Like the duct tape."

"Right," I said. "The duct tape was heavy. I get it. It was supposed to stretch you. And the magnet . . . I don't get the magnet."

"Two magnets," said Brian.

Right. There was a second one on the ground under where Brian had been hanging the other day. "Of course."

Mrs. Olsen stood in the doorway. "How can you possibly say 'Of course,' Sly? Of course what?"

"Magnets attract each other," I said. "Brian wanted the magnet on his ankle to pull his body toward the magnet on the ground. To stretch him."

"Goodness, Brian. I didn't know you knew so much science," said Mrs. Olsen.

"Nothing worked," said Brian. "I can't have fun."

"You don't need to be bigger to have fun," said Mrs. Olsen.

"Yes I do," said Brian. "I can't even hit a branch."

Mrs. Olsen looked at me with pleading eyes.

"He needs to be taller to play basketball," I said.

"Playing is the most fun," said Brian. "Sly said so. Shouting and kicking are fun too. But Kate won't let me do that either."

Mrs. Olsen looked at me again.

"He needs to be bigger to be a cheerleader," I said.

"A cheerleader?" Mrs. Olsen asked weakly.

"I don't even have pom-poms," said Brian.

If you can hit two birds with one stone, you should do it. That's what my father says. Brian wanted those pom-poms and I didn't want to be a cheerleader. "You can have my pom-poms. I don't even like them," I lied. "And you can have the best job for cheering the basketball team on."

"Really?" said Brian. "What's that?"

"Mascot."

The Mascot

So Brian became the cheerleading squad's mascot. Melody was okay with that. Her mother didn't want Pong going to the games anyway.

Kate was nice about the whole thing. She wrote MASCOT in Magic Marker on a white T-shirt and gave it to Brian. He wears it almost every day.

We had our first basketball game this week. Brian ran around with one pom-pom between his teeth, waving the other one. The crowds loved him.

I didn't get out of being a cheerleader after all. Kate's mother bought me a new set of pom-poms. It's okay, though. I really do like those pom-poms.

Mrs. Olsen paid me with another dozen cookies. I didn't know what to do with them. Then Jack came over and asked if he could have them. He has a shuffleboard game in his basement and he wanted them for pucks.

So my second set of three cases all worked out fine. The cases of the Soccer Switch and the Kick Craze and the Basketball Blues. The pairs of words didn't all start with the same letter, but they started with the same sound: ss, kk, bb. When two words begin with the same sound, that's called alliteration. Poets use lots of alliteration. We learned that in school just this year.

This was neat. My first set of three cases all rhymed. And this set all alliterated. There is definitely something poetic about sleuthing.